Seeing Off Uncle Jack

Seeing Off Uncle Jack

Bernard Ashley

Illustrated by Kim Harley

VIKING

VIKING

Published by the Penguin Group
Penguin Books Ltd, 27 Wrights Lane, London W8 5TZ, England
Viking Penguin, a division of Penguin Books USA Inc.
375 Hudson Street, New York, New York 10014, USA
Penguin Books Australia Ltd, Ringwood, Victoria, Australia
Penguin Books Canada Ltd, 2801 John Street, Markham, Ontario, Canada L3R 1B4
Penguin Books (NZ) Ltd, 182–190 Wairau Road, Auckland 10, New Zealand

Penguin Books Ltd, Registered Offices: Harmondsworth, Middlesex, England

First published 1991
10 9 8 7 6 5 4 3 2 1

Text copyright © Bernard Ashley, 1991
Illustrations copyright © Kim Harley, 1991

The moral right of the author has been asserted

Set in 14/15 pt Palatino

Printed in England by Clays Ltd, St Ives plc

A CIP catalogue record for this book is available from the British Library

ISBN 0–670–83942–6

Contents

Seeing Off Uncle Jack

Chapter 1

'He's my brother an' he ain't goin' off from nowhere but here!'

That was the start of it for Winnie, walking in from school to her mother in tears and her father looking ashamed and defiant together — the look on him that said he was sorry, but he wasn't sure he wouldn't suddenly jump in with another remark. He banged the kettle under the tap for something to do instead of putting his arm round his wife. Then he abandoned the sink area and went and put his arm round her, anyhow.

'Come on, Sugar, you're upset,' he said. 'It's natural you're upset . . .'

Winnie's mother sobbed, a sob big enough to make the man flinch for fear he was going to get poked. 'He's my only brother, ain't he? 'Course he's got to go off from here. There's no room in that flat of theirs to entertain more than their shadows . . .'

Winnie leant against the doorpost, kind of holding it up while she tried to figure what this was all about. They'd seen her, but they hadn't, sort of thing.

'Who's going off somewhere?' she asked eventually.

'Who? Uncle Jack,' her mother sobbed. 'My Jack.'

'Going where? Back home?' Winnie always referred to St Lucia as 'back home', although the Victoria Estate was all she'd ever known for herself.

'You could say "back home", Winnie, love. Yeah, he's goin' back home to heaven if it please the Lord.'

'Hallelujah!' Winnie's father gave it like a voice from the back of the church.

Winnie stood straight, left the doorpost to look after itself. 'Dead?' she asked, with the open mouth of what hardly dared be said.

'Took in the night by the good Lord.'

'Hallelujah!' Mr Stone said again, quieter this time and with reverence.

Winnie didn't know what to say. You had to be a certain age to come out with *Hallelujah!* She watched her mother work a paper tissue back to dust. 'That's a shame,' she found in the end. She touched the woman's trembling arm, and when that didn't soothe she went to the kettle herself.

Uncle Jack. Taken by the good Lord. The way her mother said it you'd almost expect to see a person floating up to heaven, like being lifted up in the sea by one of those big swelling waves you can see through, only keeping on going up and up, all relaxed, legs dangling. But not Uncle Jack! Uncle Jack you couldn't see going like that. That big man wasn't a floater, he was a sinker; she'd never known anyone so rooted to the earth. She could see him now, sitting heavy in the only seat he fitted in their flat — half the big settee — and once down he never got up. He went to the toilet before he came into the room, he sat down, and he only got up to go home. You brought him things and you carried his plates and glasses away. 'That's it, girl, while you're goin',' he'd

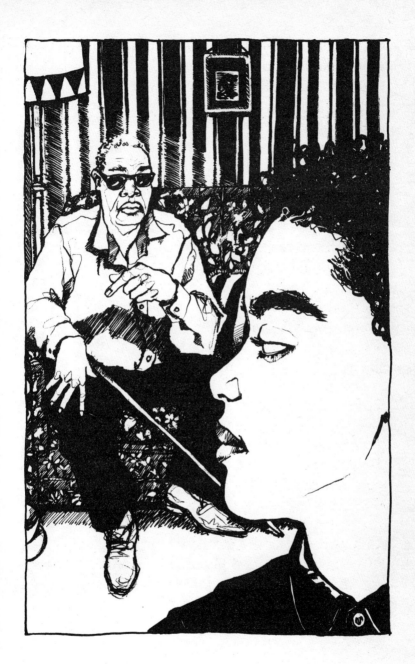

say, fumbling for his cup after watching for someone to be making a move.

Except he wouldn't be watching with his eyes, he'd be listening and feeling the air, sensing, on account of he was blind.

Chapter 2

And now he'd gone to heaven! And the kettle was running over being filled, spilling itself on the floor.

'See what you're doing, girl!' Mrs Stone always had an eye to kitchen business whatever the grief.

But Winnie's thoughts weren't on water. They were on eyes, Uncle Jack's. Could he suddenly see, she wondered, once he arrived in heaven? It would only be right: like her father having all his hair again and her mother being sugar all the time. Not that Uncle Jack had ever made a fuss about not seeing. He moaned about everything else but he never moaned about that. He'd been kind of *proud* of it when Winnie had been little. He'd show off his big watch with the lid he could flip and the hands he could feel to tell the time: and he'd get her to give him money so he could tell what coins he'd got, foreign as well. Then he'd hold out his hand for a pile of money to be laid on it, gripping at her arm and shaking it with the other hand in a sort of blind man's wink.

'How much have you give me?' he'd say, ready to come out with the answer. Then his big hand would shut and he'd lift his bum and put the cash in his back pocket. 'You've give me all of it!' And he'd laugh, throwing back his head to show that you were meant to join in, too. And sometimes it would be time for him to go home before you got the money back: but you always did, and he'd tell you the exact amount, then put an extra pound coin to it. That was her Uncle Jack, when she'd been little. But for a long time now it seemed he'd just sat on that settee in his own old world while Auntie Ren did the talking, listening while she went on about his health and the state of his bowels.

'So how is it he's going off from here?' Winnie asked, when she finally got a cup of coffee into her mother's hand.

'Because I say so and because it's right,' came the answer to a question Winnie hadn't slanted that way.

'For the funeral,' her father said. 'It has to go off from someone's house an' then come back after. And we've got the big room,' he added, going full along with it now.

'So we'll be seeing him off. Poor old Jack!' Mrs Stone looked out of the window to a view of the opposite block. 'What a terrible thing, to be deprived of your sight . . .'

Well, Winnie knew it had to be a terrible thing not to see. But to be honest, she wasn't sure Uncle Jack couldn't have been a bit more than a big man who just sat on the settee and got waited on hand and foot. There were partially sighted children at her school – OK, not blind like Uncle Jack, but Colin Wilson could only see vague shapes and he did marvels. He played the violin – had to remember all the music – and on Sports Day he came third in the three-legged with Paula Mason.

And that wasn't just her opinion of Uncle Jack, it was her brothers' as well. And when they heard the bad news they cuddled their mum first and said some nice things, but up in her room later Winnie heard them going on similar in private voices.

'Lazy old bones! Weren't never much alive to be telling the difference!' That was Danny. Danny was eighteen and everything he said was folklore. Ces, who was fifteen and shared his room, reckoned him the greatest fellow to walk the earth — when he wasn't crying over being hit by the great man.

And Winnie just knew Danny had to be listened to, even when what he said wouldn't be approved by their father. 'Never had a life worth living at all.' On the other side of the thin wall Winnie would have nodded her head, except she was frightened God would see, and she wouldn't want that bad mark on her chart. Winnie had been brought up on all the business of right and wrong: but at the age of three, when she'd started saying the Lord's Prayer, she'd got hold of *Our Father with chart in Heaven* because that's what she thought it was all about, and the idea had never really got shifted. So she pretended to keep an open mind about Uncle Jack — at least, she wouldn't let it show on her face, although she went a long way with what Danny was saying.

Chapter 3

Tight-lipped and tense, Winnie's mother and father went to see Uncle Jack wherever he was lying. They went as if they were off to a meeting, very careful about their clothes being just right for the occasion, the flower in Mrs Stone's hat not what anyone would think too cheerful. They came back with the hat in her hand and her eyes cried out, and him with his suit crumpled from where she'd held him tight round the middle.

'He looked so peaceful,' she said, and it took half an hour for her to be composed enough to get that out. 'Like he was asleep in his little bed back home.'

'He's with the good Lord,' her father said, a bit loudly to cover the pull of a fresh can of Coke. 'Yes,' he said, content, 'he's all right now.'

Then preparations started to get made for the day next week which Winnie was dreading: the Tuesday, at two o'clock from the house, when Uncle Jack would be buried. And it was in the evening while that talk was going on that Danny came standing in the doorway, not sure which way he was facing. He let out the long breath he'd been holding.

'This funeral,' he said, dropping his bomb, 'you won't mind at all, will you? But I'm not goin' to be able to make it.'

When you make a remark which has the whole

room laughing you feel like a queen or a king. So Winnie knew how Danny felt about what he'd just said – like some criminal ready for prison.

'You say that again?' their mother said, half-way between daring him and wanting a repeat.

Their father looked up from the little list he was taking down as if he was stuck for the spelling of disgraceful.

'I got my dance class Tuesday afternoon. I blow that an' I lose my solo in the Showcase. He'll know I'll think of him at the special time, Uncle Jack. You don't have to be there to think of him . . .' He was trying to get out on a weak finish and he deserved to be roasted.

'The day you're thinking of anybody but yourself is the day I'll eat my church hat!' his mother told him, getting up to say so. 'You're talking about my brother an' your uncle!' She was approaching him with her poking finger and Winnie knew he'd have to stand there and take it or lose the argument right then. And she hurt you hard, knew how to measure it just this side of a broken rib. 'An' you're goin' to be there to think of him in person, so I don't want to hear no other word about it!' Poke! poke! poke! on the last three words of her own. 'Do I?' She turned round to her husband for support.

'Should think not,' he said, a stray hand up to guard his own chest.

'I'm making up my own mind,' Danny said, and he went out ten times quicker than he'd ever come in.

Winnie went then, too. She dug out some homework she seemed to have forgotten – because what

18

she didn't want was to sit there after Danny had gone and cop it as if she were Danny, all the talk about ingratitude and Uncle Jack being family, things said and threats made only for the sake of them getting repeated along the corridor.

But the boys' room was empty anyway: Ces at Brigade and Danny anywhere else in the world except indoors. So Winnie shut herself in and put her earphones on and heard no more about the matter that night.

Chapter 4

The next night the widow came: Auntie Ren, and all of a sudden half her normal size. They'd known she was coming, and when the doorbell rang Winnie's stomach went over in a final flip of panic fright. For a start, she didn't know how to talk to her. She'd be different after such a loss, special, and Winnie was bound to say the wrong thing and have her shrieking the ceiling down in grief.

But Auntie Ren had the same voice, the same bony hold on your arm, and once the first of the tears was over, and the hugging, and the good Lording, she started talking business as matter-of-fact as if it were Uncle Jack's bowels. Winnie waited for a slight pause, like an entrant in a dance, and slipped in quick with her sorrow before the mood for it went altogether.

'I'm sorry about Uncle Jack,' she said in a rush. 'Used to like his money tricks when I was little.' It was the best she could manage.

Auntie Ren found the saddest of smiles from down in her handbag where she was rooting for another address. 'Thank you, Winnie, love,' she said. 'I appreciate that. He was very fond of you, an' all.' Then she shook her head. 'You children never saw the best of your Uncle Jack . . .'

And things moved on to talk of cars and flowers and food and drink for the Tuesday following; but

Winnie could see her chart with a good mark on it for at least saying the right thing. And before the sad little lady went home she was pleased to hear her name brought up again: a proud feeling as if links with Uncle Jack carried gold medals these days.

'He loved his little tricks, not having no children of his own. He was very fond of you,' Auntie Ren told Winnie again.

'I never knew how he done it.' Winnie wanted Auntie Ren to have this little bit extra of nice sadness.

'No, you wouldn't know about that.' She was suddenly sharp instead of sad. Winnie shook her head while Auntie Ren looked at her parents — who were shaking theirs too, but together, like a pair of windscreen wipers.

'He never would have it talked about, wouldn't dwell in the past; reckoned you caught your death on cold memories. But we was proud of him.'

Now Winnie's parents were nodding — him fast, her slow and deep — while Auntie Ren lifted her head as if she'd made a decision — to give away the treasure of a secret.

'He was your Captain Jack Sprat, down at Margate, on the front. You wouldn't remember that . . .'

Winnie shook her head, then rested her chin on her arm to show some appreciation at being told.

'"Guess Your Weight!" I took the money an' Uncle Jack stood dressed in a sailor's cap with more gold on it than the Queen's crown. An' he told 'em their weight: he eyed 'em up an' down an' felt their arms a bit, an' then he told 'em what they weighed.

21

Scribbled it on a little ticket an' give it to 'em before he sat 'em on his weighing chair to prove how he was right.'

'He did, too,' Winnie's dad put in. 'I'll vouch for that.'

'Correct to five pounds or you get your money back.' Winnie's mother was proud now the secret was out.

Winnie widened her eyes, panned them round from one to another.

'That's right,' Auntie Ren said, 'an' brilliant at that he was, an' all. Never had me giving much back, I can tell you; only to the sort of joker who'd dress up with water-wings under to make himself look fat. Even then he'd go right mostly, wouldn't he? Good judge of weight in his hand, which was how he knew your cash. But when in doubt he could tell 'em by the look of their feet . . .' She winked and chuckled as if Uncle Jack hadn't died at all.

'Is that how he done it?' Winnie's father said. And Auntie Ren tapped her nose knowingly and said, 'Aha!'

But still Winnie was staring. It wasn't any trick she was interested in. Every job and every sideshow had its trick, that was expected, especially seaside people. It was the bigger thing that had her own eyes out like ball-bearings. 'He could see 'em, then?' Her voice touched the lampshade.

''Course he could,' her mother said snappily. 'How else?'

'Oh, and we did a fair old trade, summer on summer.' Auntie Ren was sing-song now, years back with her Jack still with her, eyes bright and sparkling without the tears. 'Not for their weight, they never come crowding for that . . .'

'Oh, no,' Winnie's mother said. 'It was to meet him an' have their ticket signed personal by Jack Sprat, that's what it was all about . . .'

'Oh, yes,' said Winnie's dad.

Winnie persisted. 'So he wasn't always . . .?'

But the matter was closed, like a door suddenly shut and locked for the night. The three adults went back to a piece of undecided business about how far down the family they went with hired cars. Auntie Ren said there was definitely to be one for the two nephews and the niece: but Winnie's mother said that wouldn't be necessary, they could easily go in with one of the church folks who had a car. And she moved them quickly on to food again, because the question of Danny coming or not was still all up in the air.

Which left Winnie with nothing to do but go to bed puzzled; and to lie there with this different picture coming into her head of the man they were seeing off next Tuesday.

Chapter 5

When you're going through a family time – a christening or an illness or a wedding – that's all there is to the world. A war somewhere, or starvation, or a flood, and what you do is, you watch it on the news and then, when you open your mouth to say something, what comes out is all about you, and not them. It was like that in the Stones' flat, everything was circling round the Tuesday next. Even their church took a back seat because it wasn't their church the funeral was at, it was to be at the one nearer Camberwell, where Auntie Ren lived. As for Danny's dance class and his precious Showcase, they were nowhere in sight. It was definitely not a topic of talking – unless Danny brought it up again, and there was that warning in his mother's eye every time she looked his way that said *just let you start* . . . He might not come to Uncle Jack's seeing-off – he'd made himself plain on that – but she wasn't listening to any of the excuses behind it. So, with all the conversation being about the funeral, there wasn't much in the world Danny was saying. Just *thank-yous* for his food when it was pushed at him: and the odd *good night*. But he listened: and the evening after Auntie Ren's visit he listened to something with two eyes which didn't blink.

The reason was: Mr Quinnel came.

Mr Quinnel – or just Quinnel as he was called by Auntie Ren – was an old family friend from way back. Well, perhaps friend wasn't altogether the word, Winnie found out, but he was *someone* to them. He came from a Camberwell family and his business now was a corner-of-the-street supermarket from which he could cater for the funeral wholesale.

'Be my pleasure,' he said. 'My privilege entirely.' He wasn't a man they'd ever had in the house – he was nearer to Auntie Ren's end of things – but he came that night when he'd shut up the shop: and he'd done them the courtesy of stretching a band of black elastic round his sleeve as a token of respect.

'Captain for the day!' Ces whispered to Danny, and there was a spell of very bad coughing from the settee, silenced by a certain finger looking their way.

'There isn't nothing I wouldn't do for Jack,' the man said. 'You just say what you want and it's yours, wholesale. Just give us your list an' I'll sort it.' He was brisk to the point of being cheerful and he must have heard himself so because he suddenly dropped his voice to reverence. 'I go way back with that man, he was champeen to me.'

'An' that's why we come to you. Knew you'd be upset if you wasn't asked,' Winnie's mother put in.

'Upset?' Mr Quinnel snorted and gave a look which hinted at feelings a long way past upset. 'Why . . .' He put down his ball-point and took in a year-long breath.

'You go way back.' It was a try at a short cut from Ces, who was wanting the man to go before the football came on, wanting that ball-point picked up again and working. But it came out sounding rude and his mother turned her head so sharp she ricked her neck.

'I'll say way back. I was his manager, boy. Him and me was like that.' He showed two fingers Super-glued together.

'What, down at Margate?' Winnie tried to help Ces out.

'Lord no, girl, before all that!' He swept away Margate with the back of his hand. 'London, the West End; Number One tours; television. That's what I'm talking.'

'Television?' Winnie asked.

Chapter 6

'Don't these children know?' Mr Quinnel looked astounded, but with his eyes just a little bit afraid he might have spilled some jumping beans.

'That's all right,' Winnie's mother said. But it seemed there was a little warning there. 'Just about the dancing.'

'Dancing? And television?' Danny found it hard to keep his voice in line.

Mr Quinnel sat up taller. In a show right then he would have stood centre stage and been picked up by the star spotlight: but swivelling round on his hardback chair to address his audience he seemed to have that, anyhow.

'"Jack Sprat, the negro with brains in his feet": that was his billing. All over the country, all your big theatres. And I was his manager. Started small, see, tap-dancing competitions, won the Rest of the World up the Lyceum, then London South, your Home Counties, and All England till there wasn't a show didn't want him. Danny Kaye at the Palladium, Jewell and Warris at the Hippodrome, Billy Cotton's Band Show, your Black and White Minstrels . . .' He did a swivel to Ces, who'd coughed again. 'They even named special tap shoes after him, which he took round promoting, personal appearances in the shops, all that sort of thing.' He wagged a mark-my-words

finger. 'And he never done worse than second top, no matter who was on the bill. Name up bigger than the theatre for years . . .'

Winnie's mother had her arms folded. She didn't speak, as if it had been a fair account of her brother's fame. Instead, it was a very quiet Danny who came in; not laid back any more with his ankles crossed, but sitting up with his backbone straighter than the landing broom, and his face even straighter than that.

'Lew's got a pair of Sprats,' he said in a throaty sort of voice. Lew ran the Dance Centre.

'Oh, we sold the name years back,' Mr Quinnel told him. His voice turned mournful. 'As it goes, when Jack finished up that finished me — but I bought my little business on them shoes.' Then he brightened for the finish. 'But he was big in his time, your Uncle Jack. A very big name!'

'Yeah?' said Danny, getting up.

'Yeah!' said his mother. And Winnie read the message in that one word. *Your Uncle Jack was a dancer, boy,* it went, *an' you won't miss one blessed class to see the man off.*

But it was Danny who put the full stop to it. *'The negro with brains in his feet!'* he sneered. 'Was that s'posed to mean instead of his head?'

Chapter 7

They didn't see much of Danny after that. Those days before the funeral he was as near to leaving home as it's possible to be when you're still sleeping indoors and eating full board. But he was up and off in a mood of his own every day, and definitely written out for the Tuesday. Ces and Winnie were going in the car on their own, and Danny was going to be at a lecture he couldn't miss: that was the story, more acceptable than a dance class, even for the funeral of dancer Uncle Jack.

The Danny business threw a shadow on the shadow. Of course, Winnie and Ces and their parents knew what Danny was on about — he was upset at Uncle Jack being a show-business black of the old sort, going on with a billing like 'the negro with brains in his feet', while Danny was a dancer with all the pride of south London. But Winnie had that other question in her head. The darkest shadow of all is the dark of blindness, and she still hadn't had light shone on that.

Now, with Monday night brightening into that dreaded Tuesday and not much sleep behind her, Winnie heard the front door click as Danny did his usual exit. She had hoped he wouldn't: they had all hoped he wouldn't at the last; but there, that door had gone.

She threw herself round in bed and faced the wall where he'd been lying the other side — twisting most of the night, she'd heard him — and she pulled a witch face at where he'd been. Yeah! she knew his pride: but she knew her mother's pride as well, and she knew all right which pride should have come out on top. Things hadn't always been the way they were: people like Uncle Jack had had to put up with all sorts of dirt to get work. But Danny could easily have swallowed that pride to be at the funeral for her, for his mother. Because she wasn't seeing off Jack Sprat, she was seeing off her brother. No, Danny Stone had made one big mistake today, and he'd stopped being folk hero for Winnie.

There was no more sleep in her head any more: and going by the awake sort of coughing from her parents' room there wasn't much in their heads, either. It seemed like a cup of coffee would be welcome all round, get them started for the day. Quietly, opening her door like burgling a safe, she came out and went along to the kitchen. On the mat was the *South London Press*, new-folded as a clean sheet. She picked it up, went for the sink, got her makings together and flipped through the paper while the kettle boiled.

And it was Winnie who blew her whistle first. Like with a scalded stomach and steam in her head. *What was this?!*

There on a facing page was a short report on the death of Uncle Jack. 'Jack Sprat Bows Out' it read: and with it was a show-business picture of a thin young man waving a straw hat and flashing a big smile. And that was the shock, the picture, because Winnie had never seen Uncle Jack *looking* before: and now she did she wasn't sure she liked it. There was a canny look on him as if he knew too much; and whatever the mouth was doing the eyes were big and sad, like looking into the future. But what eventually left the coffee in the jar were the final words of the item. It had said about his dancing days of topping the bill, and his Margate days with 'Guess Your Weight', but wrapping him up and seeing him off it said, 'Jack Sprat lived his last years in darkness, after the Smuts Theatre incident, a tragic end to a talented career.'

The Smuts Theatre incident? So what was that?

Winnie must have asked her question out loud – she had lost the edge between what was open and what was secret these last few days. Anyhow, her mother came into the kitchen at the sound.

'What's all this?' she asked, looking round; perhaps hoping Danny was still about after all.

'Uncle Jack! He's in the *South London!*' Winnie twisted the paper so that her mother could see.

The woman looked, and she fell a whole lifetime silent. She read the print and she stared at the picture, and she went off somewhere else altogether. And then she lifted her poking finger and she touched the picture on the lips, as soft as feeling for a pulse. And, 'Jack,' she said, the way a mother sighs at a naughty boy at bedtime.

'Mum . . .?'

'You read this?'

Winnie nodded. Of course she had. If everyone else in south London was entitled to read it, she was.

'And?' The woman was saying she knew the question. 'That's a long story . . .'

Winnie looked at her straight. ''Long as I know 'fore I get asked at school.' And that real need could not be denied.

The mother stared at the girl while the girl stared at the paper, and finally the mother said, 'You better sit yourself down. I'm not sure how you'll take what you're goin' to hear.'

'I am nearly twelve!' Winnie sat herself down.

'An' I'm three times of that — and not sure myself how I'll take what I tell you . . .'

Chapter 8

It took a cup of coffee and a half to get Winnie's mother going, with plenty of sugar and a lot of stirring: clockwise, anticlockwise, swirls and bubbles. It was the state of her mind there in the cup, but it settled in time.

Winnie watched, and waited. She knew better than to ever prompt her mother: for a start, the woman always came from some different direction altogether. She just kept the newspaper piece there in front of them, Uncle Jack smiling out from way back before she'd been born.

'Nearly too tragic a tale to be told,' the woman began as if she were ending. But after a long last look at the picture, she lifted her head and faced Winnie and began a drumming of her fingers on the table as if to give herself a beat to march by.

'They found him, one winter, someone in the theatre world who was putting together a load of old-timers for a show. "Stars of Yesteryear", something like that, very popular them days, digging up the old acts so people could see they'd all got old as well. You got 'em on the television, their thin old voices not hitting the high notes, and their old legs doing as much shaking as dancing. And these people sugar-talked Jack, told him he could sign his own weight on the ticket, sort of thing, get paid what he reckoned he was worth, within reason. And he wasn't bad, still, no wobbly old legs from him; but of course, they had their prices all worked out.' She shook her head at the injustice of what happened. 'So they got it together, an' they did the old theatres, not the big ones no more but the picture places and the bingo clubs and the town halls, just a few weeks all told . . .'

She started drumming and talking faster now, like wanting to get to the point and safe past it.

'Then they got what they thought was the real big chance. The last chance for most of 'em, being honest. This big tour of South Africa and Australia, with money in it, good money, an' all fitting in before Jack's Margate season. So what does he say? He says yes.'

Winnie was nodding, but not fast and keen. It sounded exciting, all right, the show-business life; but they were talking South Africa, and back then . . .

'So off they went. And of course it all happened!' She showed the palms of her hands with no more needing to be said by way of explanation. And if her face had been sad for her Jack these last days, right now it was sad for mankind.

'Top and bottom of it was,' she struggled on, 'they was only letting whites in to see the show. That was the rule them days . . .'

Winnie knew. She knew about apartheid: those were lessons about the world where they didn't need medals for paying attention.

'He hadn't realized or he'd thought different some-how: definitely they didn't warn him beforehand, which they should have, because him being black in the show put one hell of a spotlight on Jack.'

Winnie's eyes didn't waver. It was all *Jack* now, without the *Uncle*, as if she were a sister, not a child.

'There was a fuss in the papers out there and back here, and the bosses said he could pull out and come home. 'Fact, he wrote to Ren saying he would. Then the next we know he's doubled back on himself and he's part of one big demonstration. All in the street, everyone shouting and dancing, and he's at the front of it in his stage clothes, blockading the whites from getting in till they sold tickets for the blacks an' all . . .'

She stopped talking, and breathing, till she drew in air like going for a dive and she plunged to the depth of her story.

'An' like these things do, it got all out of hand, an' didn't them police and them dogs love that, and the brave men in masks with their riot gas . . .'

Winnie closed her eyes.

'And Jack got it right in the face, a canister meant for a crowd. Last thing that man saw wasn't me or his mam or Ren or the flowers back home, but hate, sheer hate through the mask on that riot-force face . . .' The woman's hands had gone across her own eyes and her voice was trembling. 'Which is why he wouldn't never have it talked about. He had to live on with that look, but he didn't have to hear talk of it.' She lifted her head proudly, her eyes bleeding with tears. '"I'm me," he said. "Blind Jack, and I'm nobody else any more." He was like a wounded soldier who wouldn't talk about the war that did for him, or how he got his medals — who never wanted sighs of pity . . .'

And now Winnie was crying, too: but while hers was loud with the cry of injustice, the woman was crying softly, so silent a cry that even a blind man would be hard pressed to hear it.

Chapter 9

And who could Winnie see through her tears? Not poor Uncle Jack, but Danny. She hated him right now, had a contempt for him which was shocking and new – something to match what she'd just been told. How dare he set himself up to be the judge on Uncle Jack? What almighty right had he got not to be at the seeing-off along with the rest? And wouldn't he be *sick* if he knew what she knew now?

As if to make up for him not coming, Winnie threw herself in to help with the preparations. She Hoovered and she dusted and she Hoovered again to her mother's satisfaction. And Ces wired in, too, which was remarkable; but he probably felt the same way now he knew, although he'd never give voice against his brother.

And then the flowers started to come, and the family and friends, little posies of people in the big room; and there were phone calls from people way back, which the *South London Press* must have prompted. It kept the phone busy: otherwise if she could have found the numbers there were a few places Winnie might have chased after that Danny.

When Auntie Ren came there were more flowers crowded on their landing than she could ever have expected to see. She went limp, leaned a lot on people, before she gradually found a sort of show-business strength at the hushed babble of talk about the big man. Now everything in his past was out in the open.

The adults looked after Winnie and Ces with concern, as if they'd been Uncle Jack's constant companions. 'How sad you've gotta be, Winnie . . .' and, 'He's in the best place, girl.' 'Hallelujah! He could never have taken being old.' Which was weird, Winnie thought, considering how totally he'd taken being blind.

But worst of all, and outdoing even the fear Winnie felt for when that big car came with Uncle Jack inside it, was this great gap Danny was leaving. Everyone remarked on him not being there, till Winnie's mother and father, who'd begun by telling sort of the truth, started telling a tale. 'It's a class,' they said, making it sound all books and polytechnic. 'He's hoping they might let him off the last minute.' But Winnie knew they were throwing snowballs at the sun. One thing brother Danny was, was stubborn.

The whole flat suddenly went quiet, as if that solitary magpie flapping past their balcony had given word that the hearse was arriving. And there it was, and Winnie's mother with a sudden push she found of strict business knocked on the toilet door for Auntie Ren.

'Thank you,' came the muffled answer.

People picked up their bits, put their feet into shoes, talked in whispers while they found handbags to match their hats like some grim party game: while Winnie stole to the balcony to look at the hearse, thumping inside and catching her breath like going past a car smash.

It had nosed quietly round the corner, bringing its own dignity to the Victoria Estate. Big, its roof shining the sky back at itself, the car had flowers in the back window spelling out the letters of JACK. And as voices came to the door of the flat, the sounds of helping Auntie Ren and Winnie's father talking quietly to her mother, the catch inside Winnie wasn't for who was in that car but still a great hurting anger at Danny Stone. He should have been here for those two women, and he should have been here for Uncle Jack. And by the good Lord wouldn't he know it tonight?

They went down to the Court, Ces walking with

Winnie like bride and scared groom. And to get to their car they had to pass close by the hearse. The funeral men were piling it with flowers now, but inside, buried in the soft of all the petals, was the coffin containing Uncle Jack. From the sides of her eyes Winnie looked at it hard. It was small, a lot smaller than would have fitted the man on her settee, almost as if he was the nimble dancer again, the fit young man, the top of the bill.

The doors of the following cars clicked, were held open by men in long black coats. And at that moment some pull, some brother/sister something, had Winnie looking beyond the line of them to the jumble of parked stuff from the estate. And who was that, running through the Court as if Old Bill was after him?

Who else? Danny, in a black shirt, black jeans, with a golden carrier bag swinging in his hands.

'Danny!' Winnie cried, as if a punch had winded it out of her.

'Danny!' Her mother didn't know how to compose her face.

'They let him off!' her father told a man in a black coat.

And by now Danny was in amongst them, out of breath but shaking hands solemnly, and going for Auntie Ren, who was still nestled under the wings of her brothers. She nodded, gave a silent smile that he'd got there, and with a little frown took the golden bag he was holding out to her. Then in a humble, awkward, modest way he helped her fumble out a long cardboard box.

She knew. She didn't need help; she pulled the lid right back, went under the grey tissue, and pulled out a gleaming pair of shoes, tap shoes, shining in the sun like smiles over footlights. And on the undersides when she looked, because the proud lift of her head said she knew she should look and would not be disappointed, was the name on each sole.

Sprats.

'For putting up on the coffin,' Danny said, choking on the first word, even. 'If you like . . .'

And Auntie Ren nodded, and pressed the sole of each shoe to her lips, and gave them to her brothers to have them put there. Then she reached out her gloved hand and gripped Danny's arm, shaking it the way Uncle Jack used to wink. And Winnie's mother gave him one of those smiles a person gives maybe five times a life. Because not only was Danny here, but the world would have had to be blind not to see that those shoes were West End, and brand spanking new. Still going. Dancing all over.

And, 'Hallelujah!' Winnie said out loud.

The Princess Watch

Chapter 1

You had to keep your back straight as a broomstick and imagine the top of your head being pulled up to the girders by some invisible string. Your eyes had to look down the baths like you were staring out past the end wall. Your breath had to get held at just the right moment. And with a push down and a spring you had to throw up your arms and take off into space with all the confidence of a baby jumping to its daddy. That was diving off the two-metre board: the first part. Then you had to keep your legs straight and together and your ankles tight like they were tied with twine, so that you went into that water as if the life-guards had already made a little hole for you there. No splashing, no feet left over to make a fuss, no body landing on the surface like a fish slapped sideways into batter. Smooth, full of grace and a beautiful shape to look at. That was what Winnie Stone knew was wanted for her to stand any chance of being good enough to go in for things like medals and fancy badges for her swimming costume. That was what she was practising.

Down at the other end of the big pool Mr Jones was bending over the beginners, holding out floats and kind words. Here at the deep end Winnie was standing on the board and shivering her hands like the gold medallists do. She twisted her shoulders and took in a breath and had a quick look to see if some of the top-group kids were watching: and she couldn't help giving a little smile when Kenny Clark pointed up and started calling to her.

Of course she gave him her don't-fuss-me hand, before she held herself straight and started looking out through the far wall.

'Watch!' Kenny called.

Yeah, you do that! she thought, very pleased he was getting the others to pay attention — because this dive was going to be good; good verging on excellent. Let 'em all watch! She took in a deeper breath, then held it, felt her tummy go over the way it always did — and off she went. Push down, and . . . up! And it was *very* good, all the way to the top of the arc. She could feel how verging on excellent it was: a good even take-off, her body not throwing itself this way or that, her arms up and leading and brushing her ears. For once in a hundred springs she could actually feel her ankle bones held tight against each other: and, something she could rarely be sure of, she knew her legs were straight and beautiful. As she graced through the air she felt her face take on that cool look of someone not a millimetre out of line, tips to toes.

Only as she peeped up out of the top of her eyes at how straight those fingers were did she see it. Bangled there on her wrist like a locker band. The one thing she should never have had! Her watch. And only when she landed in a heap on the water like a shot seagull did she give up frantically trying to stop that arm going under, waving it high like

someone drowning. But keeping a whole limb dry was impossible; and there was no stopping, and definitely no going back. It was too late. Splash! The watch was probably ruined already.

Winnie had never got out of the pool so quickly. She went for the side as if the water was scalding, with the watch arm held up like the Statue of Liberty, kicking and scooping like fury and scrambling up the steps.

'Watch!' Kenny Clark called again. 'Wassup with you? You deaf?'

Winnie didn't answer; went charging for the changing room without permission.

'Mine's waterproof,' Wendy Kent had clung to the side to say. 'My holiday one.'

But Winnie's wasn't. Oh no. Hers was jewellery not sportswear, and she knew it; she'd been told it often enough. And now it was ruined: unless she'd been quicker moving than water seeping through a watch case.

Chapter 2

Winnie ran to the changing rooms shaking her wrist all the way like someone trying to get rid of a couple of fingers. Grabbing her towel she rubbed her watch in it and tried to tell herself there really hadn't been time to get any water in. But that was fancy: dreaming: and well she knew it. It was too late. As she looked hard through her crying eyes she could see already that the watch had stopped – with the hands stuck there, still as anything, fixing the time of death.

She'd tried to be too quick, that had been her trouble. She'd rushed out of the changing rooms and hurried to get to the boards before anyone else: and then she'd been so intent on showing off that all she'd had eyes for was who was watching. It had been a really stupid thing to do. The trouble was, it wasn't as if she hadn't been warned. What had her mum been saying all the time since she'd had the watch? 'That's a real watch you got there, girl, not one of these plastic toys. That's jewellery, that is, that's precious.' And along with that she'd had all the talk about not wearing it to school; not wearing it to sports – not wearing it anywhere, Winnie reckoned.

So she'd done her own thing. She'd taken it out of its jeweller's box, out of its little bed of fine brushed furry stuff, and worn it to school anyway. And the first couple of days she'd seen nothing else. She'd looked down at it ten times a minute to check on the time, she'd held her wrist this way and that way to catch how good it looked, made sure everyone in the class had seen what a fine gold watch she'd got. And she'd handed it in for gym, handed it in for games, handed it in for swimming with the school — until she'd got used to the idea of having it with her, and actually begun thinking about some other things in the world.

Now today she'd been caught out. She'd forgotten it in all her pride, and she'd got her fine piece of jewellery filled with Riverside Pool's water.

As she shook it again, flicked her wrist like a nurse with a thermometer, and checked — still no life — she heard her mother's voice sounding off in her ears, heard her deep disappointment.

'Don't grow on trees, fine things like that. Your daddy bought you that to wear dressed up: *princess* watch you got there. And now you've gone and ruined it! That's a real shame.' It made Winnie want to cry all the more, because he wasn't a rich man, her father; he'd worked hard to afford such a fine thing. And all wasted due to her stupid showing off! She could see his face, sitting there in his chair the night he'd given it, not wanting any fuss about how kind he'd been. Which made it worse, the knowing how disappointed he would be.

But that wasn't the half of it. Never mind him being disappointed, how about angry? Hadn't she been told? Wasn't she old enough to know better? Shouldn't she have been obedient?

Wendy Kent came to gloat. She must have asked

permission to get out of the water early, just to be long-faced about the ruined watch. If she hadn't known the girl better, Winnie would actually have thought she meant it.

'Does it work? Is it going?'

Winnie shook her head.

'Rotten! But they won't, not if they're not proper waterproof. My auntie had one, done what you done, only that was Benidorm. What you gonna do?'

'Get it mended. Dried out.'

Wendy pulled the muscles of her neck to make a tense face. 'Glad I'm not you.'

And at that moment, her stomach turning over with the worry of what she'd done, just for once Winnie thought she wouldn't have minded swapping places and being Wendy Kent. For a while. That was how bad she felt.

Chapter 3

She didn't say anything at home. It was Friday night and the house on Friday nights was always as busy as a bus station. Danny and Ces came in and took over every space while they got ready to go out; and her mother had a load of church business going on. Winnie could lose herself in the middle of all that activity and not get asked a single question if she was lucky. Which she needed to be — lucky. Especially not to get asked the worst single question, 'What's the time, girl?' Because with the way she'd been over that new watch they'd have noticed if she'd had to look up at the clock.

She got to bed. She took a heap of remarks for going so early — beauty sleep, boy-friends, all that sort of kidding stuff — but she managed to get to the safety of her room where she went straight for the box the watch had come in. It was one of those boxes people never want to throw away, but still don't know what to do with. It was made for giving a watch, but there wasn't much else you could do with it after. Winnie had put a couple of church attendance medals in it. Now out they came to let her get straight to the inside of the lid to find the name of the jeweller. And please let it be local! Please let it be Riverside.

But as she snapped up the lid she could see it.

Nothing. She hadn't noticed before, but there wasn't a name in it at all, none of the golden print she'd expected on the satin inside the lid. It had to be too posh for that – she could tell, holding the heavy box, feeling the way the lid shut expensively hard on her fingers.

Her father must have paid a fortune she thought, and this was just the box! Winnie put the watch back inside, had another cry as she remembered that moment when she'd first opened the lid to see it lying there like treasure, had looked up to see their faces.

She put it under her pillow while she tried to get to sleep. But sleeping wasn't easy. Her mind kept on and kept on, going through that last dive, willing it to go back to the start each time so she could do it with a bare wrist. But every dive ended up the same. Splash! And a drowned watch.

She tried sending good thoughts down through her pillow to dry out the damage, she even said prayers that a miracle could happen on the Victoria Estate and the watch would come back to life – went to sleep still listening for a ticking to come up through the pillow – but, no. No good.

She was lucky that she didn't dream that night, dreaming would have been too painful. As it was, she woke fresh and happy the next morning, and it came with a sick ache, the sudden remembering that her watch was ruined.

She scrabbled under the pillow for the box. Perhaps it had restarted in the night! The works could have dried out and got going again, couldn't they? Quartz could be a bit special like that. Eh?

But, no: there it lay, not a tick to be had no matter how hard she shook. And as she climbed out of bed on to the cold of the real floor she knew there was nothing for it: today she had to go out on a secret errand and find the shop where her father had bought it.

Chapter 4

It wasn't hard getting out of the flat. It was swimming again, she told them, well, diving – practising what she'd been learning with the school. The hardest bit was her father talking to her about not messing about running on wet tiles and all that sort of thing, and drying properly and not leaving anything behind. Him caring about her, as if she were really going. But she got over that by thinking how happy he'd be by just not knowing about a spoiled watch, and she ran all the way to Riverside, putting all her mixed-up feelings into a steady jog.

When she got there she walked up and down the High Street. It was a funny place, Riverside; her mother always moaned about it. It had jewellers galore and not much in the way of the basics like cheap clothes and good food. Its one big plus was the market near the river, where the greengrocers sold all the fruits and vegetables the Stones liked, and where the clothes were more to fashion for the bright young people of south London.

Winnie decided to start at the market end. She would go in every jewellery shop till they recognized either the watch or their own box. Well, she told herself, a watch like this, a fine piece of jewellery, they'd soon remember who they'd sold this to just the other week. Then she'd find out what they could do about repairing it, get a price for the job and see how it weighed against the money in her Post Office book. But she'd have to be truthful with them and ask them to keep her secret. With this sort of jewellery they'd probably have her father's name and address on their computer. If it was going to cost anything much to put it right, she didn't want them phoning him to get an OK on the job!

With a quick look round to make sure none of her brothers or her uncles or aunts were about, Winnie pushed the door of the first jeweller's she came to. And from that first push she wished she hadn't gone in. Even as she walked in on the wooden floor — *wooden floor*, she noticed — she had that feeling that no watch and box like these in her pocket could ever have come from here. All the cases of rings and necklaces in the tall glass cupboards had scribbled numbers all over them, and the counter had a grille across it and the man behind it needed a shave.

'Yes?' he asked, with one of those looks which said the only reason he would ever speak to Winnie would be on account of making money.

Winnie took out the watch case, already knowing she was wasting her time.

'Don't want to see it. Don't loan out to minors.'

'Miners?'

'Kids. Youth. Against the law.'

'I don't want no loan.'

'Don't buy, neither.'

'Don't want to sell. It's broke —'

'An' I don't repair.' The man was staring through her, picking his teeth with a matchstick, the burnt

end. But already Winnie was pulling open the door to the fresher air of Riverside: relieved, and knowing very well that her father would never have done financial business with a man like that.

Chapter 5

The next shop had more people in it. And it had carpet squares on the floor. It had a long counter with two or three youngish people standing serving, but it still didn't look the sort of shop which would sell the watch in the box in Winnie's pocket. It was too narrow, too cramped. But then you never knew, she told herself: they might have a special case of expensive stuff somewhere behind the scenes.

She waited her turn by the woman who seemed to be a bit over the others: the one with a suit top on.

'Do you sell these?' Winnie asked, having trouble opening the snappy box flat on her hand.

The woman was already shaking her head as they both looked in at the watch. 'Not ours, love, not a watch like that.'

Winnie looked round the shop. She wouldn't want to seem rude, but, well, she'd thought so. They weren't quite up to the standard of her father's watch in here.

And the next shop was a bit the same. It was bigger, it had more space in the middle where there was a central show-case, and where Winnie could spend some time looking round before she was forced to speak to anyone. But she didn't see a watch like hers. Not at all. Hers was called Oceeka, and it came complete with the jewellery gold bracelet, all

matching in. Those in the show-case here might have the gold on the watch, but they were all on black or white straps, and really quite ordinary. Bracelets had to be bought extra: and none of the dials said Oceeka.

Winnie looked at the boxes, too. Not that they were on show, but she saw a woman buy a watch for someone, and she was given that in a real cheap and ordinary affair. Hardly any snap to the spring of it, and very cardboard-looking. Besides, it had their shop name scrolled all over the front like a cheap advert. Time City.

She was on the point of going out when a salesman cornered her. Perhaps he thought she was up to no good.

'Yes? Can I help you?'

Winnie shook her head: but she had to make some show. 'You don't sell these, do you?' Again, she held the watch box out, flat on her hand.

The man just shook his head, making a sort of sucking sound with his mouth.

'Thought not,' Winnie said, looking round, trying hard to keep herself from sounding snobby.

He watched her all the way out: but then, she was used to that. So she turned and decided to give him a sad little shake of her head as she went, just to show how she pitied him for having to work in an inferior place like Time City.

Chapter 6

None of which was helping her, she realized. Nearly an hour she'd been out of doors, supposed to be swimming, and she'd got nowhere yet. Which was serious, because when she did find the shop, she was hoping they'd do something straight away about her drowned watch so she wouldn't be without it.

She ran to the next jeweller's. Zwars: which was known as quite an uptown place to shop. Zwars! Her aunties would sometimes talk about getting their clocks or a silver thing for cutting cakes or an eighteenth-birthday tankard from Zwars, as if the name of the shop said something really important about the thing they'd bought. Just the way her mum had been on the matter of her watch when she thought about it. *You look after that, girl — that watch came from Zwars!* She hadn't actually said it, but it fitted into the mood. After Zwars it would be Bennett's, the top brick on the chimney talking jewellers, and she could hardly imagine her father going in Bennett's unless he'd done some enormous amount of overtime to pay for it.

So she went into Zwars with a certain feeling of *This is it! Here we go!*

The door was heavy, the carpet was thick, and he was a very nice assistant, treated her a little bit like she was off the telly. Very nice! He looked like

Linford Christie only in a suit, and he came round the counter very smooth, sort of through it, and he didn't fall over himself to serve her, just arrived.

'Yes, madam?'

Well, that was different to being treated like a beggar or a thief. And he gave her all his attention while he talked to her, wasn't looking over her head for somebody else going into the till.

Oh, yes! She could just picture her father getting excellent service for his money in here, and being very pleased to spend a few pounds over the odds to be served so dignified. Without looking round for watches or matching boxes, Winnie had a very strong feeling that she was on the winning stretch in Zwars.

'Had an accident with this.' Again, the box was made to snap open and sit on her hand. 'Took it for a swim, and it don't.' Winnie smiled. 'Don't swim. It stopped straight off.'

The man took it and looked at it carefully, as if it were the Queen's. Winnie could tell he knew a fine piece of jewellery when he saw it. He dangled it on its bracelet, shook it for water behind the glass, but not too violently.

'Reckon you'd be looking at a replacement,' he said after some thought. 'These modules hardly ever repair.'

Replacement? He didn't mean he'd give her one on some sort of insurance, did he? Nothing marvellous like that?

'How much?' Never mind the wet in the watch, Winnie couldn't keep the water out of her mouth.

'I wouldn't know, madam. Perhaps where it was bought?'

'Oh. Not in here, then?'

The salesman pursed his lips, shook his head. 'I'm sorry, not.'

Too grand again! Winnie let the box snap shut, just prevented it jumping off her palm and on to the floor.

'And a beautiful box you got there. But not one of ours.'

Winnie nodded, thanked him, went to pull the door open but he was there first, doing it for her, smiling a bit like a doctor who has just had to refer you to Harley Street.

'Ta,' she said.

'OK.'

So, it was Bennett's, then. The best jewellers in Riverside. And now when she thought about it, what she'd really been coming to think all along, was that her father had gone to town in a big way on the buying of this watch. Only the best for his Winnie! And what a stupid, thoughtless kid she'd been! Because the trouble was, hand in hand with the watch being so dear was the knowing how much more of an arm and a leg this was going to cost to sort out. If Zwars wouldn't repair, she could be as sure as money not growing on trees that Bennett's wouldn't either.

Chapter 7

It took Winnie a while to actually get into Bennett's. Not because the door was expensive and heavy — although it was both — and not because the shop was crowded out with customers — because it wasn't — but on account of the *thought* of the place she was going into.

It was the sort of shop which you really wouldn't call a shop. It definitely didn't look like one. All they'd got in the window, apart from a little spotlight, was a necklace on a draped velvet cloth: and, of course, there wasn't a hint of a price to it.

It took a fair bit of plucking up courage, then, going in there. First, for the going in: then for finding out the worst. Which would certainly be, no, they couldn't repair the watch, and no, her Post Office money wouldn't come anywhere near to buying a replacement. She could almost see the snooty smile on someone's face, taking pity on her as she walked out of the shop and tried to keep her back straight.

Back straight! Winnie suddenly stood up tall. Back straight! She knew about that. Back straight, head up, grace and line: that was what she'd had to learn in diving. So, she knew how. How to dive in! And how to show the same courage that those first headers off a board had called for. Now all at once she had it — the guts to go in. Well, see some of these snoots going in off top board, she told herself, they wouldn't get their feet half-way up the ladder. They'd be the sort who suddenly turn back with a load of excuses and go off to splash down the shallow end.

But not her. Winnie pushed the door and went in. Her first sentence dried on her lips, though: the one she'd prepared. There was no one in there, just a carpet like the Grand Hotel, a desk, and three low swivel armchairs. And all there was on show was one display of jewellery hanging as if it grew on its miniature Japanese tree.

The manager didn't speak, she coughed. She came from nowhere and she coughed, part of that special language of sounds and looks which sales-people use. And she smiled, just the mouth, and chucked her head up in a little jerk which seemed to ask, 'Yes?'

Winnie went into the same language. She smiled back, just the mouth herself, and held out the jewellery box flat on her palm again.

With a little twist of a 'pardon me' face the woman lifted the watch and held it up for scrutiny, with just a hint that it could have been a drowned mouse. And she laid it back into the box with a smart little shake of her head and a wrinkling round the eyes.

Winnie didn't know what the woman imagined she was after: whether she wanted to sell it, have it valued, repaired, pawned, engraved; the bracelet expanded, shortened, polished; the clasp fixed, a safety chain added; or the whole thing melted down and made into a set of gold teeth for biting her with. She just shook her head. And in the move she'd rehearsed outside, Winnie snapped the box shut and walked on two steady athlete's feet across the carpet and pulled at the door.

She had almost got round it when the woman actually spoke.

'Try the market, love,' she called in a very ordinary voice. Not posh at all.

Winnie twisted her head and stared in surprise: turned it into a mean look: tried to slam the door on the rude woman. But doors like Bennett's won't have slamming. And anyway, the woman had already disappeared back where she'd come from.

Chapter 8

After a long session of diving the legs go weak. It's all the springing, and the tension of holding them to a position in the air. It's never a good idea to go for a distance swim after a long session of diving because that's when cramp can strike.

Now a certain sort of cramp had struck Winnie: but not in the legs. They'd gone weak all right, but the cramp was mental, like a lack of blood to the brain. She did feel light-headed, which could have been rushing out without breakfast: but it was much more likely to be the insult she'd just heard from the woman in Bennett's. Try the market! What a cheek!

At first she wondered whether she should put her head back round the door and shout something nasty. But two things stopped her from doing that: one was the lack of something dead right to shout — she'd just sound rude and stupid; the other was the tone there'd been in the woman's voice. Because it hadn't been snooty. What she'd said had been out of order all right, but not the way she'd said it. That had almost sounded kind . . .

Winnie walked back along the High Street, her eyes on the pattern of the herring-bone paving. He could have got the watch up West, she thought, in London: gone up to Regent's Street after work one night. Or he might have gone to Brent Cross one

Saturday afternoon. It had to be something along those lines if it wasn't Riverside. But what good was knowing that? She wasn't going to be getting to either of those places in a hurry, was she? She was stuck with a drowned watch here in Riverside High Street. And she was fixed with a family who'd be asking all sorts of questions about this watch if she stopped wearing it while she searched the world for its shop.

By the time she had decided there was going to be nothing for it but a confession and a whole lot of sadness around, Winnie found herself back at the market end of the High Street. And, seeing the stalls and hearing the shouts, she decided that she'd just wander through − on her way home. There was a skinny hope, just a skinny one, she thought, that there was a man in the market who could give her watch a look, repair it even − give her five minutes more time than the people in the shops and actually take the back off it. Then perhaps she wouldn't have wasted the morning altogether . . .

Head down, definitely last-hoping, Winnie threaded through the market. Past sweet-smelling fruits, over rotten cabbage leaves, through racks of bright party frocks, getting caught in a queue for bananas − and keeping her hands still and her eyes aside while a salesman knocked out Sony Walkmans as cheap as cotton wool. But at last her eyes lifted at a man who sold watches.

Jarvis. Cheap Jackie Jarvis, Jwllr, who was eating a cheese and pickle roll and had a pint of beer on the go, selling stuff between mouthfuls − all very different

to the Bennett's style of things. But he had a kind face, on the young side of being old, and Winnie thought he was the sort who would at least give the watch a look.

Once more, out came the box. And once more, there it sat, flat on her pale palm.

Chapter 9

'What's up with it?' Jackie Jarvis asked, tearing at a piece of roll which wasn't sure whether it was coming with the mouthful or staying. He didn't put a hand out towards the watch, regarded it from where he was leaning.

'Got water in,' Winnie said. 'Went swimming in it.'

'Oooh.' Now the man did take it, fished it out of the box as if it wasn't precious at all, sort of tossed it in the air while he got it where he wanted it one-handed in front of his eyes. He shook it roughly, then threw it down on to the cheap pad of black velvet he had in the centre of the stall. 'Got plenty of water resists,' he said. 'What you fancy, Swatch style, or what?'

'I don't want a waterproof,' Winnie explained. 'I want that one mended, if you can . . .'

The man didn't even consider it. He drew in one of those 'impossible' breaths, shook his head, coughed on a skin of pickle. 'These don't repair, not these. These bin.'

'Been? What you mean? Where've they been?'

'*Bin.* In the bin. Chuck 'em. Buy new.'

Winnie coughed on nothing. 'But that's precious!' she said. 'That's jewellery. You can't chuck that away.' Help us, this was crazy talk, this man couldn't have

74

any idea the hours her father would have had to work to buy her a birthday watch like that.

'Nice box,' he said. 'Anyhow, if you're stuck on the watch, you'll have to bin this and get another.' And still using his one free hand, while the other now went for his beer, the man flipped the drowned watch back at Winnie and started lifting and tapping a show-card standing prominent on his stall. It was so prominent, Winnie wondered she hadn't seen it before: seen it, or seen what was written on it, or seen what was lying there in front of it.

£5 was what was scrawled in felt-tip on the card. And what was lying there in front of it were three rows of Winnie's watch, all shining golden against green felt and dropped cheese crumbs.

Winnie bent down and looked hard. 'What are these? Cheap imitations?' she asked. But even while the man shook his head in his beer she was knowing. She was looking hard at the name on the face and at every detail she could. Oceeka. And the answer she was coming to was that if these were cheap imitations, they were good enough to fool anyone short of a watchmaker.

And one of them would definitely be just the article to take back home on her wrist.

Chapter 10

Winnie Stone wasn't stupid. She was old enough now to know a little bit about the world. She was old enough to know that everything wasn't just the way it looked. She knew enough of things which happened at Victoria School to know that the tale the teachers heard wasn't always the way it was. She knew enough to know that certain things which she read in the local papers weren't always written up the way they'd really been. So she guessed she knew enough to know where her father had actually bought her birthday watch.

She went home from the market sitting on the bus with a sort of permanent shrug in her shoulders. It was in answer to anyone around who might have asked her the question.

So, he'd seen the watch in the market, and he'd liked the look of it, knew she would, too. The cost of it probably hadn't come into it. Cheap or dear, it was the watch, the look of it that had been important. Then he'd found that nice box somewhere else, to set the whole thing off. But he hadn't lied. He hadn't put the watch in a box saying Bennett's or Zwars, had he?

And as she went on thinking about it, hadn't it been her mother who'd done all that *jewellery* talking, all that *princess* stuff? Her father hadn't. As far as Winnie could remember, all he'd done was sit over in his chair and smile a bit goosy.

The bus stopped at the Victoria Estate. Winnie jumped off, suddenly lighter, happier. Its being jewellery hadn't mattered to her; what had mattered had been its being a present from her parents. And she'd got it back now: well, got another one similar: so they weren't going to have to be disappointed about her getting the first one wet, were they?

She looked at the new watch, very pleasant on her wrist: gleaming with the same golden lustre. She lifted it up to her ear the way she'd done for two days solid with the other one: and there was that expensive — well, that efficient — tick. She ran the bracelet down her cheek: felt it still smooth and comforting. Yes, everything was back to being right. From now on, when she thought about Riverside Pool, it could be with diving in mind, and not with a drowned watch and a disappointed father.

With a little skip in her step she ran up the flights and rang on the doorbell to her flat. She'd just have to be careful, she told herself, not to start talking about swimming as if she hadn't already been that day. She hitched the collar of her shirt, blinked her eyes to water them like the chlorine did.

But the way her mother opened the door told Winnie she'd have had to get up early to pull one over her. As she stood there with one straight arm holding the woodwork wide, Winnie knew the game was up. Even so, she went past giving the sweetest smile a girl could ever give a mother. But her wrist suddenly got held up so high her feet started to leave the ground.

'Swimming?' her mother boomed. 'With this on

your arm?'

'No!' Winnie said. 'Yes! What I'm meaning is . . .'

'What I'm meaning, young lady, is what are you doin' wearing this precious piece of jewellery to a swimming pool with *water* in it?'

Winnie tried to picture one without. The water, that was. But this was no time for putting any humour into the air.

'Your daddy's told you, an' I've told you, and what are you still doin'?'

Winnie knew the answer to that. So she gave it, quickly. 'Wearing my watch. But I take it off for the water . . .'

'Oh, yeah?' Winnie's mother led her through, still gripping her by the watch wrist, took her on her tallest toes into the living-room where her father was sitting up in his armchair, very stern-looking: and very little-boy-looking, too, with a long straight back.

'That's not what Mrs Kent's been tellin' me! Wendy's mum. That's not it at all! That lady's been tellin' me about a certain girl who doves off the board and gets her watch all wet under the water. That's what I've been hearin'.'

'Dives. It's dives, not doves.'

'Don't you correct me! It's watches we're talkin', not English literature!' And still without loosening her grip on the arm, Mrs Stone lifted the girl's watch to her ear, to listen for the tick.

Winnie stretched, went with it: the only thing to do before she was suddenly let go, back to her own gravity, staggering a moment to keep her feet.

'Well, thank the good Lord for that! You got it fixed.'

All Winnie could do was nod. Yes, she'd got it fixed. The problem, that was — not the watch. She'd have been happy to leave it at that nod, too: go on using the language of the woman in Bennett's, because this was one of those times when words would have to say too much.

'An' where was that, then? Hope you haven't cost yourself a fortune, girl? Dearer the item, dearer the mending, that's been my knowledge, and that's a real princess item you've got there.'

Winnie looked across at her father. He was staring back like someone with a hand in a mousetrap down the other side of his chair.

Winnie went from him to looking at her mother. Both of them too precious to have an upset over what he had or had not spent on a watch. *They* were the real jewellery round here. Crown jewels. Her mum was the princess, and her dad was the prince. And she wanted the watch still to be the wonderful thing it had been before anyone had made any bones about how much it had cost.

This header had to finish without any splash — and without telling a word of a lie, either.

'The lady put me right in Bennett's,' she said. 'And no charge.'

'Bennett's! Oh!' Mrs Stone turned round to her husband with one of those special big smiles she saved for his birthday and Christmas: even more impressed than before.

But he just made a noise in his throat and gave a leaky old smile across at Winnie: another time when it was best not to use the language of words.